Elsewhere Editions
232 Third Street #A111
Brooklyn, NY 11215
www.elsewhereeditions.com

Funding for the translation of this book was provided by
a grant from the Carl Lesnor Family Foundation.

This work was made possible by the New York State Council on the Arts
with the support of Governor Andrew M. Cuomo
and the New York State Legislature.

Archipelago Books also gratefully acknowledges the generous support of
Lannan Foundation, the Institut Ramon Llull, the National Endowment
for the Arts, and the New York City Department of Cultural Affairs.

PRINTED IN CHINA

GUSTAVO ROLDÁN

Juan Hormiga

TRANSLATED FROM THE SPANISH
BY ROBERT CROLL

If there was one way in which Juan Hormiga was second to none, it was his way of taking a nap.

Well, I should say naps, for he took six or seven every day. And that's just if it was a normal day. But if it was raining, or even if the sky was simply cloudy, then the thing really turned serious and he could take as many as ten naps in a single afternoon.

A-JUMMM...!!!

In this way, he'd earned a certain fame for laziness around the anthill, yet the other ants didn't mind too much, for Juan Hormiga had one other ability: he knew by heart each and every one of his grandfather's adventures from the days of his youth.

Juan Hormiga's grandfather had been the bravest creature to ever set foot in any anthill, the most intrepid, the one who'd made the longest journeys and traversed lands beset with the greatest dangers any ant could face.

Juan Hormiga knew all of those stories, and he knew how to tell them, and, best of all, he could do it just as if he'd lived through them himself.

Whenever he crossed paths with another ant, Juan Hormiga would say something like this:

—Hello there, ant, did I ever tell you about the day when my grandfather escaped from the eagle's talons? He leapt from the very top of a poplar tree, holding tight onto a leaf.

At that moment all of the others would turn their heads, put down whatever they were doing, and come closer, one by one, drawn to Juan Hormiga's colorful narration and the extraordinary escapades of his grandfather. For a while, the whole anthill would forget about work and give in to his hypnotizing words.

And so the days went by in the anthill.

One morning, Juan Hormiga surprised all of the others, not just because he'd woken up early, but because he was holding a stick between his feet with a little cloth bundle full of food.

—I'm going away on a journey, said Juan Hormiga, raising his voice high so that everyone would listen.

And, to make sure that no one held any doubts as to his intentions, he added:

—I'm going to follow the paths my grandfather once traveled. I've told his stories too many times now, so I've made up my mind to go out and see the world, and when I return, I'll have heaps of new stories to tell.

And on that note, calling out: See you soon, my friends, Juan Hormiga sprang out of the anthill and set forth upon his march.

The hours went by.
An almost nocturnal silence hung over the anthill.
One ant asked:
—Where will Juan Hormiga be now?

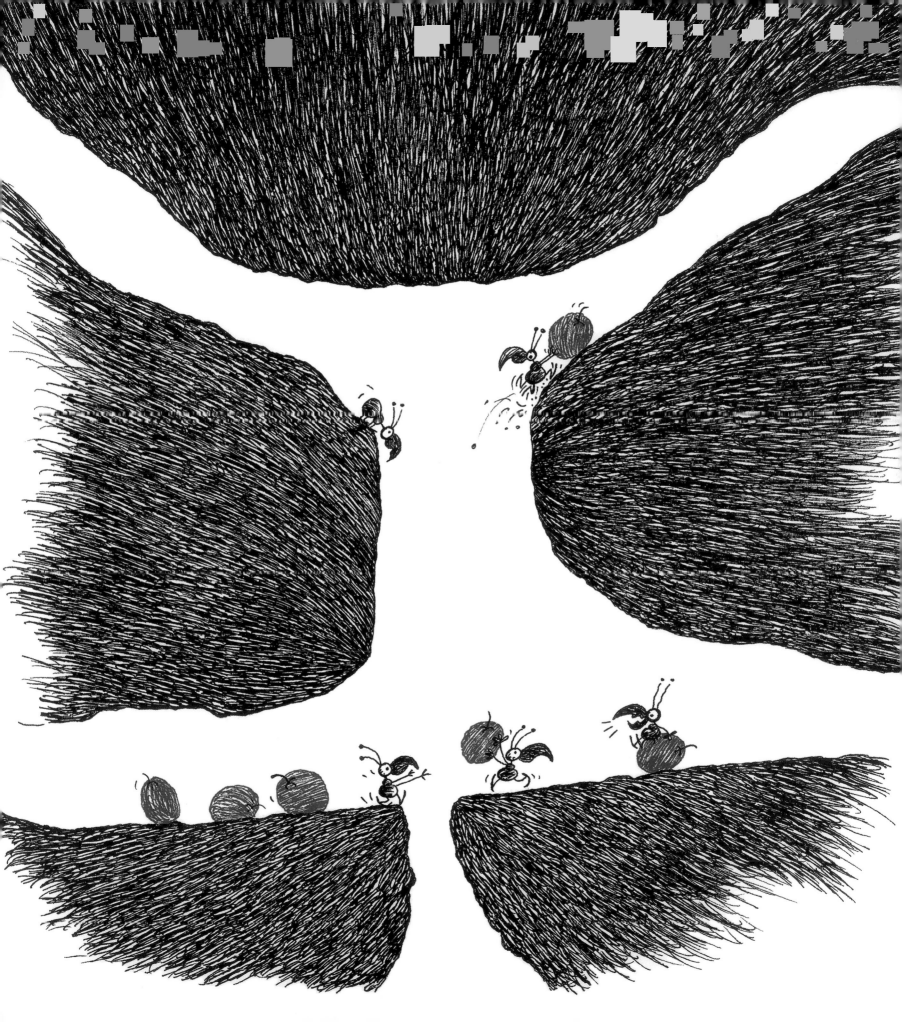

And another one responded:

—By this time, he must be coming to the river.

And another added:

—He'll surely try to ride across it on a branch, just like his grandfather did.

And one more pointed out:

—You'd have to be terribly brave to do that. That river is far too strong for an ant.

Then another ant ventured:

—Maybe he's going down into the ravine, hanging from a spider's thread. His grandfather did that too.

And another observed:

—You'd have to be very strong to do that. If you weren't tremendously strong, you wouldn't even last a minute hanging from a spider's thread.

And…

—How brave Juan Hormiga turned out to be. So brave and so determined.

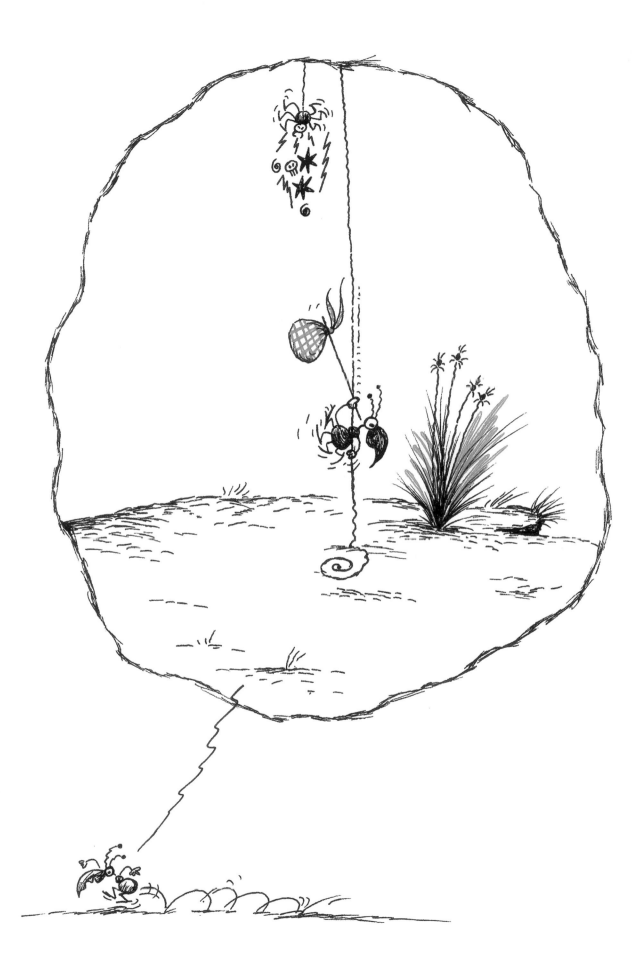

Distracted by their talk, the ants didn't notice that everything was being covered by heavy clouds, laden with water. Then a clap of thunder burst in the sky and gave way to rain that flooded everything as fast as I'm telling it now.

The ants scrambled up to the highest point of the anthill in search of refuge.

—If the water moving past our anthill is so strong, it must be much worse in the river.

—Much, much stronger. The river turns into an angry beast when it rains.

—And that's where Juan Hormiga was beginning his journey.

—Yes. And he also said he was thinking of plunging into the river from the top of the giant willow tree that stands on the bank, just like his grandfather once did.

—If he was thrown into the water, the current must have swept him away.

　　—And he'll be drowned. Poor Juan Hormiga.

—Poor Juan Hormiga. As brave as he was, to meet an end like that.

—A hero through and through. Juan Hormiga was braver than anyone in this anthill since his grandfather.

In the meantime, the rain had stopped and the water had drained from the ground, leaving a sticky sludge at the foot of the anthill.

The ants took a moment of silence in homage to the valiant Juan Hormiga.

—Let's plant a flower in his honor at the foot of the great willow tree, one ant proposed.

Without wasting even half a second, off they went, marching, marching, in search of the giant willow tree that grew on the bank of the river, bringing with them the prettiest flower in all the land and bearing a sadness as great as the tree they were heading toward.

—Where are you going with that flower? asked a passing mosquito, flying alongside the expedition of ants. And why those long faces?

—We're going to pay homage to our friend Juan Hormiga. We'll plant this flower in his memory.

—Why? Has Juan Hormiga lost his memory, perhaps?

—No, Mosquito, in memory of him: Juan Hormiga's been swept away by the river.

—Juan Hormiga? But I saw him just a moment ago. He's sleeping in a knothole in the giant willow tree.

The ants broke out into an uproar:

—He's survived! Did you hear that, boys? Juan Hormiga survived the flash flood.

—He must be wiped out, he must have passed out from exhaustion after swimming so hard against the current.

—And dodging the tree trunks being dragged along by the water.

—The flash flood must have pushed him all the way up to that knot in the willow.

The troop of ants picked up their step, and a moment later they were standing beneath the giant willow tree.

—PSST! Hey! Juan Hormiga, wake up!

—Do you need help getting down? Surely you have no strength left.

—Yes, you must be keeling over.

Juan Hormiga cracked open his eyes and murmured: Mmmmh? What's going on?

—Hey! My friend, are you okay?

—Of course I'm okay. What's all this shouting about? answered Juan Hormiga.

—What courage you have, Juan Hormiga, after everything you've been through.

—And you act like nothing happened. What a courageous ant.

There was Juan Hormiga, upright, unscathed, and so unconcerned. So much so that the other ants' antennae quivered in surprise.

 —Why shouldn't I be okay? said Juan Hormiga, stretching.

 —We took you for dead, but here you are, you've survived.

 —Survived what?

—Look! He still has his bundle of food, one ant pointed out. And he doesn't have any mud on his feet. He's completely clean.

—Of course I'm clean. I've always been the cleanest kind of ant.

—But after everything you've been through, you should be all covered with mud.

—And all covered with bumps.

—I've only taken a nice nap in this comfortable knot in the trunk of the tree, my friends. As far as I know, no one gets dirty from that.

—And the flood? You didn't get swept away in the flood?

—What flood?

—So you didn't swim against the current until you were exhausted?

—No flood, no current, none of that. I only took a nap. As soon as I reached the foot of this willow tree and saw that the clouds were growing heavy, I climbed up here to take shelter and drifted off to sleep.

The ants looked up at Juan Hormiga from the ground, dumbfounded.

And a little disappointed as well.

Juan Hormiga tossed down his little cloth bundle and sprang after it, flipping through the air like an athlete, and then, landing on top of this improvised cushion, he said:

—Since we're all here, and since it doesn't look like it's going to start raining again, let's sit down and eat all of this food I have in my bundle. Meanwhile, I'll tell you about some of my grandfather's amazing feats one more time.

Indeed, the rain did not start up again that afternoon.

And there the ants remained, nibbling on delicacies, listening for the hundredth time to the dangerous adventures of Juan Hormiga's grandfather on the day he escaped from the eagle's talons, leaping from the very top of a poplar tree, holding tight onto a leaf that served as a parachute.

En mi casa no hubo televisión hasta que cumplí los diez años. Aparte de jugar con mis amigos del pueblo y los largos paseos en bicicleta por el campo, lo que recuerdo con más cariño de esos tiempos son las noches de los viernes y los sábados, sentado junto a mi hermana a los pies de la cama de mis padres. Entonces mi padre nos contaba historias, sobre todo historias de animales, mezclando recuerdos de su propia infancia con cosas que improvisaba sobre la marcha. Mi hermana y yo nos divertíamos como locos.

En los veranos, entre ríos y bosques, acampábamos en la montaña. Durante el día pescábamos, nadábamos y haraganeábamos a gusto. Por las noches hacíamos un fuego y nos sentábamos alrededor a escuchar a mi madre, que nos leía *las aventuras de Tom Sawyer*.

Juan Hormiga es un pequeño homenaje a todas aquellas noches que tengo grabadas a fuego en mi memoria.

—Gustavo Roldán

Until I turned ten, there was no TV in my house. Apart from playing with friends in town and taking long bike rides through the countryside, what I remember most fondly from those times were the Friday and Saturday nights spent sitting beside my sister at the foot of my parents' bed. My father would tell us stories, especially stories about animals, blending memories from his own childhood with things he made up as he went. It was crazy fun for my sister and me.

In the summers, among rivers and woods, we'd go camping in the mountains. During the day we'd fish, swim, and lounge around. At night we'd build a fire and sit around listening to my mother, who read *The Adventures of Tom Sawyer* to us.

Juan Hormiga is a small homage to all of those nights that remain seared into my memory.

—Gustavo Roldán

I grew up in a house with a red tin roof that stood on the side of a small mountain. Almost everyone around there had dogs and let them run free, and so they socialized much more than the people. One of my neighbors was a great puppeteer, and on certain afternoons I'd walk up the hill to learn music or the names of plants from him while my mother was giving his daughters math lessons.

These days, if I'm not wondering about stories like the ones Juan Hormiga tells, I'm probably making lemon cloud pancakes or writing quiet, angular songs for the guitar. I also like to take photographs that show spaces built by people (but with no people inside) and that seem to change the longer you look at them.

—Robert Croll